Ladybird Read

The Gingerbread Man
Activity Book

Written by Catrin Morris

Song lyrics on page 16 written by Pippa Mayfield

Illustrated by Virginia Allyn

 Singing *    Reading    Speaking   Critical thinking

 Spelling    Writing   Listening *

Look and read. Write *a* or *an*.

1 ...an... old woman

2 .... gingerbread man

3 .... cow

4 .... oven

5 .... horse

6 .... fox

2 Look at the picture and read the questions.
Write the correct answers.

1 How many gingerbread men is the old woman making?

She is making one gingerbread man.

2 Where is she putting the gingerbread man?

....

3 How many cups are behind the old woman?

....

4 What color is the woman's dress?

....

3 **Work with a friend. Talk about what's in your room. Use *There is* and *There are*.**

1 There is a little bed in my room.

2 . . . on my wall.

3 . . . under my window.

4 . . . next to . . .

5 . . . behind the . . .

6 . . . on the table.

4 Match the two parts of the sentence.

1

The old woman was
happy because

he was
hungry.

2

The old woman was
angry because

she made a
gingerbread man.

3

The fox ate the
gingerbread man because

the cow wanted
to eat him.

4

The gingerbread man was
frightened because

she could not catch
the gingerbread man.

* To complete this activity, listen to track 2 of the audio download available at **www.ladybird.com/ladybirdreaders**

Work with a friend. Ask and answer questions about the pictures.

1

> What did the old woman do?

> She made a gingerbread man.

2

> What did the gingerbread man do?

3

> What did the old woman, the cow, and the horse do?

4

> What did the fox do?

Look at the pictures. Put a **in the correct box.**

1

a gingerbread man ✔

b gingerbred man ☐

2

a hoven ☐

b oven ☐

3

a little old woman ☐

b little old uoman ☐

4

a caw ☐

b cow ☐

5

a hose ☐

b horse ☐

6

a foks ☐

b fox ☐

8 **Read the questions. Write the answers using the words under the pictures.**

old woman   fox

cow   horse   gingerbread man

1 Who wanted to eat the gingerbread man?

The cow, the horse, and the fox.

2 Who made the gingerbread man?

3 Who ran from the house?

4 Who ate the gingerbread man?

9 **Read and write the sentences.**

The little old woman	ran from	the cow.
The gingerbread man	put	the little old woman.
The horse and the cow	said	the gingerbread man in the oven.
The fox	ran in front of	the gingerbread man.
"I want to eat you,"	ate	the fox.

1 The little old woman ...... put the gingerbread man in the oven.

2 The gingerbread man ....

3 The horse and the cow ....

4 The fox ....

5 " I want to eat you," ....

10 **Listen and put a** **in the correct box.** *

1 Where did the old woman put the gingerbread man?

a  b  c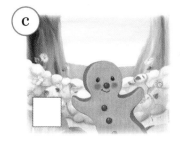

2 Who did the gingerbread man meet first?

a  b  c

3 What was the girl's favorite part of the story?

a  b 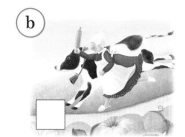 c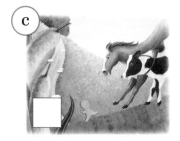

4 Where was the gingerbread man?

a 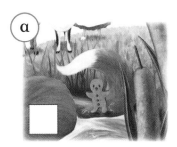 b 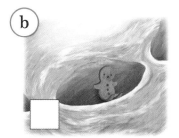 c

11 **Read and write T (true) or F (false).**

1 The little old woman put the gingerbread man in the oven. ......T......

2 The little gingerbread man ran in the house. ....

3 The little old woman did not catch the gingerbread man. ....

4 The little gingerbread man met the cow. Then he met the horse. ....

5 The fox wanted to help the gingerbread man. ....

6 The fox ate the gingerbread man. ....

12 Choose the correct words and write them on the lines. 📖 ✏️ ❓

cow

tail

horse

fox

back

head

cup

bowls

These are animals:

cow, horse, fox

These are parts of an animal:

You eat and drink with these:

13 Read and complete the words.

ee   oo   oo   ss   tt

1 She put him in the oven to c oo k.

2 The d........r was open.

3 "Stop, little gingerbread man!" said the li........le old woman.

4 "I can help you to cro........ the river," said the fox.

5 "My f........t are in the water," said the gingerbread man.

14 Find the words and write them on the lines.

hioro**ven**otrriverpeskpocatchcredhorsergcowhsgingerbreadmansoitailfstbackwifoxcas

1 _oven_

2 ....

3 ....

4 ....

5 ....

6 ....

7 ....

8 ....

9 ....

15 Sing the song. *

"Stop!" said the woman. "I want to eat you."
The gingerbread man ran and ran.
"Stop!" said the cow. "I want to eat you."
The gingerbread man ran and ran.
"Stop!" said the horse. "I want to eat you."
The gingerbread man ran and ran.

He ran to the river, and he met a fox.
"I must cross the river," said the gingerbread man.
He jumped on its tail. But his feet were in the water.
He jumped on its back. But his feet were in the water.
Then the fox said, "Jump on my head!" . . .
And he ate the gingerbread man!

* To complete this activity, listen to track 4 of the audio download available at **www.ladybird.com/ladybirdreaders**